For Kate and Sam —D.L.

To all of the "kids," Corey, Luke, Brianna, Sara, and Johnny —J.N.

Text copyright © 2012 by David Levinthal
Illustrations copyright © 2012 by John Nickle

Visit us on the Web! randomhouse.com/kids

Educators and librarians, for a variety of teaching tools, visit us at randomhouse.com/teachers

Library of Congress Cataloging-in-Publication Data
Levinthal, David.
Who pushed Humpty Dumpty? : and other notorious nursery tale mysteries / David Levinthal ; illustrations by John Nickle. — 1st ed.
p. cm.
Summary: Police detective Binky investigates the theft of a golden goose, the poisoning of Snow White, and other fairy tale crimes.
ISBN 978-0-375-84195-8 (trade) — ISBN 978-0-375-94595-3 (glb)
[1. Fairy tales—Fiction. 2. Characters in literature—Fiction. 3. Detectives—Fiction. 4. Humorous stories.] I. Nickle, John, ill. II. Title.
PZ7.L57968Wh 2012
[E]—dc22
2009048808

The text of this book is set in Aaux Pro Medium.
The illustrations were rendered in acrylic on paper.
Book design by Rachael Cole and Becky Terhune

MANUFACTURED IN MALAYSIA

10 9 8 7 6 5 4 3 2 1

First Edition

WHO PUSHED HUMPTY DUMPTY?

AND OTHER NOTORIOUS
NURSERY TALE MYSTERIES

DAVID LEVINTHAL
ILLUSTRATIONS BY JOHN NICKLE

schwartz & wade books · new york

GOLDILOCKS

There are eight million stories in the forest. This is one of them.

It was a typical Sunday morning for the Bear family. They had gone out for a walk while their porridge was cooling.

I was working the robbery detail out of the Pinecone Division. My name's Binky. I'm a cop.

The call came in at 12:15 p.m. It was Mrs. Bear, and she was upset.

"Officer Binky! Officer Binky! Look at our house! Someone's been eating our porridge and sitting in our chairs and sleeping in our beds! We found her snoring away when we came home. Luckily, Baby Bear scared her off."

I calmed them down, and then I started to look for clues.

A strand of blond hair,
an empty porridge bowl,

blue cloth on a broken chair,

and a rumpled quilt.

I'd heard that story before. It could
only be one dame: Goldilocks! I nabbed
her trying to make her getaway.

Down at the station, she confessed. "I was hungry and tired," she said. They'll feed her three meals a day where she's going, and she'll have plenty of time to rest.

HANSEL AND GRETEL

You get all kinds of people coming into a police station. Some are crying, some complaining. But until today I had never seen one come riding in on a broomstick.

"I know my sister is a witch. I'm a witch and our mother was a witch. But she is still a person—well, at least, sort of. And she's been missing for over a week, so I want someone to look for her!"

Binky, I said to myself, this isn't going to be your day.

I took down the information. The sister wore black, had a large pointed hat and several warts, and lived deep in the woods in a cottage made of candy. Oh, and she loved to cook. That should narrow it down, all right.

I took the patrol car and drove out to Deep Dark Woods, an old housing development at the edge of the forest. If there were witches to be found, this was where they would be.

They didn't call it Deep Dark Woods for nothing. No one lived here now; there was just a cottage that belonged to an old woodcutter. I knocked on the door.

"I knew you would come someday," said the old woodcutter.

He called to his children, "Oh, Hansel, Gretel! Come in here, please. We have to tell the officer what happened."

I listened to their sob story. Once upon a time, the family had no money, no food. So the kids' stepmother had an idea. She told their father Hansel and Gretel had to go.

And go they did—deep into the woods, where Stepmom and Pop left them.

"We really didn't mean to eat that house we found," Hansel said.
"But we were so hungry."

"We would have helped fix the roof we ate, honest," chimed in Gretel.
"But all that witch wanted was to fatten Hansel up like a pig for dinner.
"When she leaned into the oven to show me how to light it, I slammed
the door shut!
"Then I grabbed Hansel out of his cage and we ran as fast as we could."

We all took a walk into the woods. I saw the witch's cottage, or at least what was left of it. There were some pretty plump animals roaming around nearby, and a few bears that will be visiting the dentist soon.

It looked like a clear-cut case of self-defense. "Kids," I told them, "just stay away from houses made of candy, or you'll be sitting in a dentist's chair next to those bears." Which reminds me, I think I'm due for a cleaning.

HUMPTY DUMPTY

It was a quiet morning in the forest. The sun was coming up and the birds were singing. I had just settled into my chair at the station when the phone rang.

"Binky, my boy, I have some bad news."

I knew the voice right away; it was my old friend from the forest, Harry Wolf. He had moved to the City years ago and joined All the King's Horses and All the King's Men, Humpty Dumpty's band. Boy, could that Harry howl.

"It's Humpty. He's fallen and gone to pieces and I don't think All the King's Horses and All the King's Men will ever be able to put him back together. He'll never play those drums again."

Harry Wolf wasn't someone who cried for help unless he really needed it. I packed a suitcase and took the next bus.

On the way I had time to think about old Humpty. He was a good egg—always called to say hello on my birthday.

When the bus pulled into the station, Harry was
there to meet me, along with the band. We were
at the scene in no time.

Harry was right, it was a mess. There were
pieces of eggshell everywhere.

I looked up at the wall, where it seemed Humpty
had been sitting. Did he fall, or was he pushed? It was
hard to tell, but one thing I noticed was that there was
almost no yolk on the ground.

It seemed odd. That much yolk couldn't go far. So I decided to walk around the neighborhood.

HAM-N-EGGS

I hadn't gone two blocks when I spied an omelet stand. A pig in a chef's hat was flipping eggs. A lot of eggs, if you asked me.

I took him downtown for some questions. It wasn't long before he confessed. He knew his bacon was cooked.

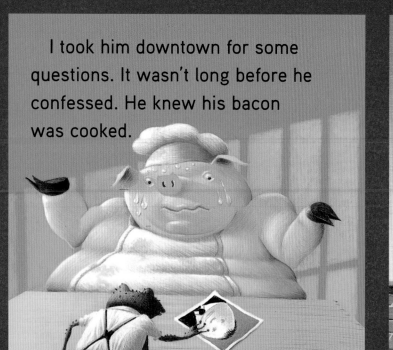

"Honest, Officer, I only wanted to ask Humpty to let me join the band. But he said pigs couldn't sing, only oink.

"That's when I lost my temper and gave him a push."

The good news was that we had our pig, and he was on his way
to a different pen.
The bad news is that All the King's Horses and All the King's Men
is short one wild and crazy drummer.

SNOW WHITE

The Queen visiting the forest! For everyone else this might be a
thrill. For me, Officer Binky, a veteran cop, it was just another day
on the job.

I knew her the moment I saw her; I think it was the crown.

She was coming to judge the annual Forest Beauty Pageant.

"They say I'm the fairest in all the land," she announced to the
press guys. "So who better than I to judge a beauty contest?"

The pageant would have the usual contestants: Elsie the cow, Henrietta the pig, and that sweet girl who cleaned for the Seven Dwarfs. I think they called her Snow Flake—no, Snow White.

I saw Snow White once. Boy, what a knockout! Better-looking than any queen I ever saw. I figured she was going to win first prize and that new refrigerator.

I kept wondering, though: Why was the Queen always talking to that big mirror she carried around? Especially since she always seemed to be yelling at it.

It brought out the cop in me, and I decided to follow her.

Imagine my surprise when I saw her dash into Ye Olde Costume Shoppe.

When I caught up with her later, the Queen sure didn't look like herself.

"Of course I'm in disguise!" she explained. "If people know I'm the Queen they always ask me silly things like 'Do you know Cinderella, and is she really as nice as she seems on TV?'"

"What's with the fruit?" I asked.

"Why, it's just a gift for that sweet Snow White," she replied.

I let her go, but the cop in me was still suspicious.

The morning of the beauty pageant arrived, and Snow White was nowhere to be found. Then a 911 call came in. It was from one of the Seven Dwarfs—Dopey. I didn't even know he could use a phone.

"Snow White is asleep and we can't wake her up. I think something terrible has happened!" he cried.

I got to the Dwarfs' just as they were wheeling the poor girl into the ambulance.

Inside the house, the first thing I saw was an apple core by the bed.
I sent it to the boys down at the crime lab.

Nobody looked more shocked than the Queen as Snow White arrived
for the Forest Beauty Pageant that night.

When I asked Snow about her quick recovery, she said, "My doctor
was such a prince! I felt better the minute he touched me. In fact,
we're engaged!"

Later, the boys at the lab handed me their results. It was the Queen,
all right. Poisoned apples. I should have guessed.

While I put the cuffs on the Queen, she blamed the whole thing on
the mirror. "He kept telling me I wasn't the fairest in all the land! He
said Snow White was! I had to do it! Don't you understand? I had to!"

Honey, looking at you right now, I think the mirror got that one right.

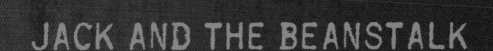

JACK AND THE BEANSTALK

There's nothing quite like the sounds of the forest. So peaceful you almost can't help falling asleep.

I was settling into my Saturday-afternoon nap when suddenly there was an enormous CRASH!, and the ground shook like in an earthquake.

A moment later, the phone rang.

"Binky." It was Lieutenant Crib. "There's been an explosion somewhere near Olde Market Road. Get right over there."

I hopped into my patrol car and sped off.

At the scene, I'd never seen such a mess. Next to a little cottage was a huge hole in the ground, leaves and branches all over the place.

Just when I thought it couldn't get any stranger, I saw a kid running around with a goose under his arm and—you're not going to believe this—a basket of golden eggs! Carrying on to beat the band was some woman—must've been the kid's mother.

"Oh, Jack, I was so worried about you! Why did you climb up that beanstalk?" she cried.

I sat them all down and tried to get the straight story. The kid started going on about how he'd traded his mother's cow for some magic beans.

The mother piped up. Like any sensible dame, she'd thrown the beans out the window, and then this morning—voila! One big beanstalk!

Now it was the goose's turn to talk. Even with all her honking, she made more sense than that kid and his nutty mother.

"You see, Officer," she began, "many years ago I was kidnapped by an awful giant.

"He took me up to his castle in the sky and forced me to lay golden eggs for him, day in and day out.

"Then this morning, something exciting happened at last. A boy came to rescue me.

"I told the boy we'd better leave quickly. But the giant saw us and started yelling 'Fee! Fi! Fo! Fum!' I can't tell you how many times I've heard him scream those words before catching some poor fool and eating him.

"Jack picked me up and we ran for the beanstalk, the giant hard on our trail. Fortunately for us, he was clumsy. He tripped on the first branch and went crashing to the ground. What's left of him is in that large hole over there."

Now I knew what had caused that explosion and the earthquake. Of course, getting the lieutenant to believe me would be a whole different story.

I took a deep breath. "Okay, Goldie, let's you and me go down to the station house," I told the goose. "Lay a couple of those golden eggs on the way. We're going to need proof."